A LIFT-THE-FLAP BOOK

CATCH UP, LITTLE CHEETAH!

Michele Coxon

Happy Cat Books

For Tim and Toni with love

Text and illustrations copyright © Michele Coxon, 1999

The moral right of the author/illustrator has been asserted

First published 1999 by Happy Cat Books, Bradfield, Essex CO11 2UT

Reprinted 2000

A CIP catalogue record for this book is available from the British Library

ISBN 1 899248 28 5 Paperback

ISBN 1899248 23 4 Hardback

Manufactured in China

Also by Michele Coxon in Happy Cat Books

The Cat Who Found His Way Home

The Cat Who Lost His Purr

Kitten's Adventure

Kitten Finds a Home A Lift-the-Flap Book

Look Out, Lion Cub! A Lift-the-Flap Book

Where's My Kitten? A Hide-and-Seek-Flap Book

Who Will Play With Me?

"Little cubs, today you must try to run fast," says Mother Cheetah.

They all run after mother, but
Little Cheetah can't keep up.

"Rest here by the trees," says Mother Cheetah.

This is a pretty
place to rest.

"Hello Gorilla,
can we play?"

Who's that staring at me?

"I can see you..."

Oh, its raining!

"You termites do work hard."

I'll sit on this log.

Little Cheetah runs like the wind from the hungry crocodile.

"Well done!" purrs Mother proudly, "you can run very fast…"

Little Cheetah sleeps in the moonlight resting on her mother's warm fur.